Confessions of a

Nerdy Girl

Diary #3

LETTERS FROM SUMMER CAMP

by Linda Rey

www.NerdyGirlBooks.com

ISBN: 978-1-949557-07-7

Cover art by www.fiverr.com/Nizar86

Summary: A socially awkward girl shares the experience of her first sleepaway camp in heartfelt letters to friends and family back home.

To see all of the Nerdy Girl Books by Linda Rey, go to
www.NerdyGirlBooks.com

For Crystal

CONTENTS

July 19, 5:01 P.M.

URGENT!

Dear Dad,

I just got off the bus, and there seems to be some sort of terrible mix-up regarding this ~~summer camp~~ PRISON!

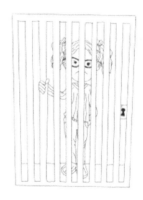

The brochure that I reviewed and approved was for SCIENCE CAMP. I repeat, SCIENCE CAMP!! I don't know how or why, but I have somehow been imprisoned in a **SPORTS CAMP!!!** And not just your average, minimal effort, everyone-gets-a-trophy-for-breathing kind, but a worldwide, la-di-da, Olympics-bound one!

Am I being punked? This seriously CANNOT be what you intended — the most uncoordinated, non-athletic girl in the universe trapped in a camp for phenoms and future Nike endorsers. Are there like hidden cameras and microphones around recording me as an unknowing contestant on a survival show? You know the kind, it's where the clueless sap struggles to survive with limited resources and supplies in a hostile environment while their unshaved legs begin to resemble a gorilla's and their teeth grow moss from a lack of proper dental hygiene.

Because that's what it will be like if I'm forced to stay here for five weeks!! With my underdeveloped lungs, flabby muscles, and lack of physical robustness, I won't last four days before I'm airlifted to the nearest hospital because of malaria or a strained muscle or something.

If I'm not being punked, then is this some sort of "tough love" thing that parents do, like when they lie and say "this won't hurt a bit" before tearing off your Band-Aid along with three inches of your epidermis?

I know the divorce has your world turned sunny-side over, but I can't believe for a second that you held the science camp brochure in one hand and the sports camp brochure in the other and said to yourself, "Gee. Camp Mauch Chunk: Fostering Athletic Excellence, seems like a perfect fit for my trips-over-her-shoelaces daughter."

Not to be a "wisenheimer" as you like to say when I'm being sarcastic, but do I need to REINTRODUCE myself to you?

I'm your daughter, Willa Shisbey. Remember her? The glasses-wearing, all-thumbs, two-left feet, physically dyslexic, OCD nerd — WHO THOUGHT SHE WAS GOING TO SCIENCE CAMP!! I repeat, SCIENCE CAMP!

PLEASE CALL THE OFFICE IMMEDIATELY TO RECTIFY THIS GROSS MISTAKE!!!

I'd call you myself, but the PRISON GUARDS masquerading as camp counselors have confiscated my cell phone. As for their excuse of, "There's no cell service in the mountains anyway," I don't believe that for a hot second. It's northeastern Pennsylvania, for gosh sake's, not Mars. Surely, there's a cell tower somewhere within fifty miles of here. And why they won't let me email you is nothing short of anarchy. I've heard of "going off the grid," but this is ridiculous! No phones. No computers. Puh-lease!

I'd send smoke signals because that's how urgent this letter is, if I thought you'd be able to see them, and assuming I had internet access to get a quick tutorial on how to make them (I think it requires some green wood and leaves and a blanket or something.)

But as I mentioned, I DO NOT have internet access or a computer or a phone! So please reply ASAP! If not by return letter, then by carrier pigeon or Pony Express. ANYTHING that will quickly resolve my EMERGENCY!!

Yours in athletic peril,

Willa

CAMP NEWS

July 19, 9:30 P.M.

Dear Dad,

I know I just wrote you four hours ago, but on the chance that you get THIS letter before the first one, please don't bother writing me back. Instead, please call the office ASAP and tell them that Grandma died (They don't need to know it was 20 years ago.) so you can claim "Emergency" status, which is apparently the only way I'm allowed to talk to you.

There has been a GINORMOUS MISTAKE!

I DO NOT BELONG HERE!!!!!!!!!!!!!!!!!!!!!!

CALL ME!!!!

Love,

Willa

CAMP NEWS

July 19, 9:46 P.M.

Dear Marley,

Hi. How are you? I hope this letter finds you doing well. It's only been 36 hours, 22 minutes, and 15 seconds since we last saw each other, but I already miss you TONS!!!

I MISS YOU! ... I MISS YOU!

I don't know what I was thinking when I agreed to go to camp!

I'm not kidding. This place is a NIGHTMARE! Seriously, on a scale of 1 to 10, it's a MINUS 5! (It would have been a minus 10, but they gave us some freshly baked chocolate chip cookies when we got off the bus. They were fab!)

If I know you, and I think I do, right now you're saying to yourself, "Just how bad can it be?" My question to YOU, Marley May, is how much time do you have?

First, let's start with the "amenities" or lack thereof.

1. No cellphones. ("Supposedly," there is no cell service up here, and our phones were literally STOLEN from us for "safekeeping" as soon as we arrived.)

2. No computers. (For us anyway. I'm sure the office has one to promote the fraudulent propaganda of this place and for emergencies and stuff.)

3. No television. (Although Friday night is "movie night," but who knows what lame old-fashioned flicks they'll surprise us with. My guess is it's G-rated oldies, circa 1990s, and rear projected from a reel-to-reel tape and onto a white bed sheet suspended between a couple of pine trees.)

4. My "home," if you can call it that, for the next five weeks, is a CABIN IN THE MIDDLE OF THE FOREST, not even a complete cabin, but just four wood plank walls with a measly canvas covering for a roof. Basically, I'm living in a tent. (And in the off chance you've forgotten about my struggles with OCD, you can probably guess how I'm feeling about now.)

And the clincher is that my bed is a bunkbed!

Which means that I AM LITERALLY sleeping in the same virtual space with a complete and TOTAL STRANGER! Talk about Stranger Danger! I'm 36 inches away from someone who could be an "America's Most Wanted" for all I know. For that matter, ANY or ALL of my eight "cabin mates" (plus one counselor) could be full on looney tunes! That's nine total strangers who I have to live with for the next five weeks. The whole experience is giving me major PTSD and bringing back in full HD detail my awful years at the orphanage. I swear, Mar, if I'm forced to share a tub with these girls, like I had to do with the kids at the Children's Home Society, I'm gonna have a major meltdown.

And Marley, the smell of the cabin! Oh, my gosh. It is so GROSS! Way worse than the girls' locker room at school, and you know how bad that was! (Imagine the dirty sock/B.O. thing of the locker room and then add dead mouse, deer poop, and burnt marshmallows, and you'll be close to knowing how bad my cabin smells.)

As if all of that wasn't enough to show how much of a MISTAKE it is for me to be here at Camp "Mauch Chunk," which means "Mountain of the Sleeping Bear" in the Native American Munsee-Lenape language, here's the clincher...

Are you ready for this?

It's a SPORTS CAMP!!

Yes, you read that correctly. Not a science camp like my dad said, but A SPORTS CAMP. And not one where you go to LEARN how to do things, like play ping pong or shuffle board or whatever, but one where you go to "hone your Olympic skills," according to the mission statement printed in GIANT LETTERS on the wooden sign at the entrance.

And just in case you think I'm exaggerating as usual — I promise, I'm not!

Everyone here is already some sort of "champion," which begs the question how my application slipped through the cracks. (Unless the Spelling Bee now qualifies as an Olympic sport!)

Two of the girls in my cabin, twin sisters named "Independence" and "Liberty" (Yes, those are their real names.) hold the NATIONAL RECORD for the fastest 50- and 100-meter freestyle swimming in their age category. And not to sound super judgy, because I've only known them for less than a day, but "Indy" and "Libby" sort of creep me out.

Remember that scary movie we watched at your house last summer, "The Shining," and the scene with those two ghost girls? Well, Indy and Libby are "dead ringers." (Pun intended.) Believe me, the image of the Grady sisters and their soulless eyes is NOT the thought you want rolling around in your mind at night when you're lying awake in the middle of the forest with the sound of wolves howling all around you. (OK. They MIGHT be coyotes, but as far as I'm concerned, a coyote is just a wolf that hasn't reached its full potential.)

Another girl in my cabin, Charlie, (which is short for Charlene — and not to be confused with her brother, who is also a Charlie — but short for Charles and in the boy's tent across from us) is a Level 8 Regional Gymnastics Champion from Texas, and she trains at the same gym as Simone Biles! Yes. "THE" Simone Biles. So far, Charlie seems normal, but it's early in the game.

Amyfromatlanta (I kid you not, the girl introduced

herself as a complete sentence.) has the bunk beneath me (She lost at rock-paper-scissors.), and she's the captain of her school's Lacrosse team. (Lacrosse? Is that the thing that looks kinda like badminton? I was too embarrassed to ask.)

Zoya, or maybe it's "Zara" (She has braces, and you know how sometimes people with braces have a lisp?), is on some pre-Olympic superstar soccer team that recently won the National Championship.

We also have a girl in our cabin who goes by the name of Suzy-Q. And don't let the cutesy name fool you. Suzy-Q is a black belt in one of the martial arts. (I forget which one. Kung Pao, maybe.)

Emma is a Mauch Chunk "lifer," according to her. This is her fourth consecutive year. Emma is six-feet-tall and is considered a "phenom" (also according to her) at both basketball AND volleyball. (And for good reason, because she's almost 12 inches taller than everyone else, so she definitely has a "leg-up" on them. HA!)

Prisha's sport is field hockey, and Harper's (who is from northern California so everyone in our cabin thinks that we should know one another) sport is soccer. Or maybe it's reversed. Maybe Harper is field hockey, and Prisha is soccer. Honestly, all those "grass sports" seem the same to me.

We also have a cabin counselor, as I've mentioned, and she wants us to call her "Gopher." I gotta say, Mar, I really admire her bravery because she has these huge front teeth, and it's hard not to make the comparison. Do you think she just wants to get ahead of things? You know — by stating the obvious?

I gotta go for now. It's time for "bunk inspection," whatever that means. (But you know me. If there IS one thing I'm good at, it's neatness, so I don't anticipate a problem.) I'll write you later.

Love,

Willa

P.S. Can you give me some tips on how to make friends? (You know, how I hate to be the "conversation starter!") Like, do I just walk up to kids and say HI? Or do I say "Yo?" or "What's up?" and then do that head toss thing that Cody does that I find to be so cute? Are handshakes appropriate? Please advise.

July 20, 1:32 P.M.

Dear Cody,

How are you? Are you having a fun summer so far? (I know I've only been gone a few days, but a day in camp life is an eternity!) Are you and your brothers getting in a lot of "surf time?" Say hi to them and give Dude a kiss for me. (To clarify, I'm referring to Dude, your dog — not that guy at the beach who you call "Homeless Dude," the one who hangs out by the pier and bums for spare change.)

Cody, remember when you told me that I'd like "Smarty Pants Camp," as you put it?

As I recall, you said, "Chill out, Willa. It's Smarty Pants Camp. It has your name 'written all over it'." Only this is NOT Smarty Pants Camp after all. OH, NOOOOO.

Instead it's—

A SPORTS CAMP!!!!!

(OK. You can get up off of the floor now. And please stop laughing before you wet yourself.)

That's right. Your friend Willa is now a prisoner of a **no-pain-no-gain, let's-get-sweaty, feel-the-burn, I-think-I'm-gonna-puke** Sports Camp!

Before you say, "How Totally Awesome!" or "Rad!" or any of those cute Cody-isms that you do, let me tell you that this is not a camp where everyone is a noobie at sports and they came here to learn for the very first time how to jump, block, pass, pitch, throw, vault, hurtle, or whatever it is that you sportspeople do. Oh, no! This is a camp where you "hone your Olympic greatness," according to my bunkmates.

Now I'm sure you're wondering, how I, the girl who can't get from first to second period at school without getting winded, have somehow found myself at a sports camp geared for Olympic hopefuls. That makes two of us. So far, it remains one of the world's great mysteries — right up there with why a slug has four noses, who was Jack the Ripper, and why kangaroos can't fart. (For reals. They can't. Look it up.)

Let me fill you in on some of the details about what happened after I got off the bus from New York City to Nowheresville, USA. (My first solo plane ride from Cali to NY was fun, but I'll fill you in on all of that the next time I see you.)

After we all arrived and were assigned our cabins and put our stuff in our bunks (Yes, Cody, I am sleeping in a tent/cabin and sleeping in a bunk bed!! The world has now stopped spinning on its axis.), we were herded inside the main rec room for what our counselors called "Orientation."

Only it wasn't an orientation at all! It was this lame, over-the-top re-creation of the opening ceremony of the Olympics, complete with a runner carrying a "torch." (Or, in this case, a large waffle cone filled with orange streamers to simulate fire instead of a triple scoop of vanilla or Rocky Road or whatever, the usual cone fare.)

The camp counselors and instructors each wore the uniform of their specific sport, and they circled the room while getting all RAH-RAH! GO, TEAM, GO! on us. It was then that I realized that a huge mistake had been made. Surely I must have gotten on the wrong bus and been sent to the wrong summer camp. So while everyone was going all, *U-S-A! U-S-A!* cray-cray and whooping and hollering like they'd just won the winning numbers in the Powerball jackpot, I hightailed it out of there, and I ~~ran~~, ~~jogged~~, ... (Who am I kidding?) ... I **"ambled"** to the supervisor's office to explain how I was the victim of a huge mix-up and how I needed to be put on the next bus headed south towards La Guardia airport.

But do you know what headmistress Trunchbull said?

HA!

(Remember, Trunchbull — the evil headmistress in the movie, "Matilda"? And how she was also a former Olympiad and did the shot put, the javelin, and the hammer throw?)

So, anyway, Trunchbull, our camp director, whose real name is Terri Trimble but looks EXACTLY like Trunchbull and even won a bronze in shot-put in Sydney in 2000, told me that even though MOST of the campers at Camp Mauch Chunk are "PHYSICAL SPECIMENS OF STRENGTH AND ENDURANCE," that there were a few of us who were granted "SPECIAL CONSIDERATION" in the hopes that our time at camp would reveal a hidden "talent," so far unrevealed. "Unrevealed talent," my eye! Unless arranging the contents of my closet by color and sleeve-length gradation is an unrevealed talent, there is NOTHING to reveal.

Cody, my take on all of this is: (A.) My dad dropped the ball and didn't get my application in on time to qualify for Science Camp, and this was the only camp still available.

Or (B.) My dad dropped the ball and didn't get my application in on time to qualify for Science Camp, and this was the only camp still available.

(Ha!)

There is also a (C.) that I don't want to consider, and it's that Diane, my adoptive mom, hated me so much that this is some sort of twisted payback for not being the cute normal daughter she thought she was getting when she and my dad adopted me.

Oh! I gotta go. It's time to line up for something or other. (There's a lot of that here.)

Willa

P.S. I know we're taught not to hate, but I hate it here!!

July 20, 5:47 P.M.

TO: The Occupants of Arendelle

FROM: Willa Shisbey

RE: My Underwear

Dear Bunkmates,

Whoever stole all of my underwear,

please return them!

Thank you,

Willa

P.S.

FYI, unlike all of yours, my name is NOT printed inside on the label in black permanent marker. Somehow, I did not get the memo that it was NECESSARY to label underwear that I've owned for quite some time now and could easily identify as mine. Plus, the Sunday, Monday, Tuesday,

Wednesday, Thursday, Friday, Saturday thing is a pretty solid identifier.

(And in case you are wondering... I own a SECOND pair of Tuesday.)

CAMP NEWS

July 21, 9:31 P.M.

Dear Olivia,

If this was a phone call, I'd be saying, "Please don't hang up!" but since it's a letter, I'll say:

Please Don't Rip This Into A Million Pieces Before You Read It.

First off, I'm sorry.

So sorry...

I'm sorry that your mom and my dad are getting a divorce. And I'm also sorry just now for using the words "my dad" when I know that he's actually YOUR REAL DAD, and he's just my adoptive dad, as you've reminded me a zillion times. (But as I like to say ... he sure feels REAL

31

to me! … **FYI:** Your mom?? Not so much.)

I'm also sorry that I wasn't pretty or popular or had long blond hair like you. I'm sorry that I was born with a cleft palate that gave me the scar above my lip that grossed you out and that I wear "nerdy glasses," as you call them. (I'm sure you noticed that Dad has the same frames???) I'm sorry that I annoyed you because of my H-SAM, that Highly Superior Autobiographical Memory-thing that I have that allows me to remember every day of my life with computer accuracy. I now see how crazy it must have made you when I'd spout off my former daily cereal selections by month, day, and year, just to show off…

May 1, 2017: Fruity Pebbles … May 2, 2017: Fruit Loops … May 3, 2017: Apple Jacks… (Who says boxed cereal isn't healthy? Look at all that fruit!! Ha!) … May 4, 2017: Lucky Charms … May 5, 2017: Muesli (I'm sure that even you remember when Dad made that Muesli, and how gross it was, and how we both dumped it down the garbage disposal, and then how Dad gave us another bowl because he thought we liked it so much.)

I'm sorry that I came into your life without you having a say-so and that you never liked me.

I'm sorry.

Love,

Willa

P.S. I hate camp. I have to sleep in this tent thing with nine other girls, and you know how much I need "my space."

CAMP NEWS

July 22, 1:35 P.M.

Dear Marley,

Ugh! Camp is so lame.

LAME... SO LAME...

Today at breakfast in the "Grub Hub" (picture the school cafeteria, only more rustic, and where everyone is tall, gorgeous, and athletic — except for me), we were told to "put on our thinking caps" and come up with an overall theme from where we'd choose our individual cabin names. I raised my hand and suggested that we go with the 12 Greek Olympiads, which, duh! makes sense since it IS a sports camp after all, and everyone here except for me will someday have their face plastered on the front of a Wheaties cereal box because they won like a million medals or something in some Olympics.

I then explained that we could take our pick from the Olympiads: Zeus, Hera, Poseidon, Demeter, Athena, Ares, Apollo, Artemis, Hermes, Aphrodite, Dionyses, or Hades.

But NOOOOOOO.....

Apparently that's "Too Obvious," according to Skunk and Muskrat, the two counselors from the cabins next to mine. As I've mentioned, the counselors get to choose their "Spirit Animal" names. Skunk's real name is Shelly, and she has shoulder-length hair that's black from the roots to her ears and then it's blond from the ears down. Muskrat's real name is Mia, and I have no idea if she resembles the animal because I wouldn't know a muskrat if my dad filleted, breaded, and cooked one for dinner.

Instead (and get ready for this!), it was voted that we had to name our cabins based on a "Land" or "Kingdom" from a Disney movie!

If that doesn't scream fifth grade, I don't know

what does!

And, Mar, you'll die laughing when I tell you what kingdom I'll be forced to live in for the upcoming cold and possibly icy five weeks.

Arendelle!

Yes, Arendelle, from "Frozen." So, of course, since it was voted 8-1 for Arendelle (I was the 1. It would have been a 9 to 1 count, but counselors aren't allowed to vote.), now all my cabin mates are going around singing "Let it Go!" at the top of their lungs. Yuk. I think my ears are bleeding.

No lie, it's like hearing a choir made up of a flock of geese, a dozen crows, and a cat with its tail stuck in the door. (Those girls may be athletic, but they are terrible singers!)

Mauch Chunk has 10 sleeping cabins in total, five boys and five girls for the campers, and a few others that are for the staff. Here are the 10 goofy names (Ha! Accidental Disney joke there) that the kids came up with in addition to the movies that they're from.

Boys' cabins:

1. Wakanda: (From "Black Panther")

2. The Dark Kingdom: (From "Tangled: The Series." I know, weird, right? — That boys came up with a kingdom from such a girly show. I guess it's a lesson not to genderize movies.)

3. Pride Lands: (From "Lion King")

4. Sugar Rush: (From "Wreck-It-Ralph")

5. Mount Olympus: (From "Hercules" — Obviously SOMEBODY liked my original idea!)

The girls' cabins are:

1. Arendelle (I don't need to explain.)

2. Narnia (Ditto)

3. Pixie Hollow: (From "Peter Pan." It's where Tinker Bell lived. And it will come as no surprise that most of the girls in Pixie Hollow are gymnasts and each girl weighs about 12 pounds.)

4. Atlantica: (From "Little Mermaid." Lots of swimmers in that cabin.)

5. New Gumbria (From "Adventures of the Gummy Bears.") FYI: I never saw the movie. I like to eat Gummy Bears, not watch them, unless it's watching them disappear inside my mouth!

I've included a map at the end of this letter so you can see where I'm living for the next five weeks.

Tomorrow, those of us who don't have an assigned sport start our "circuit training." Instead of being humiliated in one sport, I'll get to be humiliated in a bunch of them. We haven't even started with the hard stuff, and I already have shin splints because of all the hills. And the air is so thin up here, Mar, that it's hard to breathe. Gopher says that I'll get acclimated pretty soon.

I'll write you again tomorrow and let you know how it went.

Give your mom and dad a hug for me.

love

Willa

PRISON MAP

(My cabin is the one closest to the archery field—
and just a few feet away from the **Forest of Death**.)

CAMP NEWS

July 22, 9:38 P.M.

Dear Dakota,

How are you and Dallas? I'm sure you are having a fun summer shopping at the mall for cute "twinning" outfits. Is the "dressing alike" something that's a lifelong requirement for twins?

Not trying to be a jerk or anything, just asking.

I hope you don't mind that I'm writing to you, especially since you basically hate me, but there's a saying that Gopher — she's our cabin counselor, and SHE chose her "spirit animal name," which I find to be quite courageous and is a story for another day! Anyway, Gopher says, "Absence Makes the Heart Grow Fonder," so I thought I'd put the theory to the test and see if the very thought of me still makes you want to puke (which you might remember is the last thing that you said to me before summer vacation started. Remember how when I said, "Bye, Dakota. Have a nice summer. Maybe we'll run into each other at the beach." And you responded with, "I hope not, Willa, because the very thought of you makes me want to puke.").

In case you were wondering about the stationery or why the return address label says Pennsylvania, it's because I'm at summer camp in northeastern Pennsylvania. (I'm sure you recall from that geography test that we had last year — you got a D if I remember correctly, and you joked and said D actually stands for "Delightful!" — that the state of Pennsylvania sits just below Transylvania and is slightly east of Ohio.)

HA!!

I am totally kidding about Transylvania. Transylvania is in central Romania and is where Count Dracula was from. We do not have vampires up here, but we DO have werewolves. (At least, that's what boy Charlie said. Boy Charlie is girl Charlie's brother. Girl Charlie is in my cabin, and her brother is in the cabin next to us. Boy Charlie said that he saw a werewolf a few years back during the Night Hike, but girl Charlie thinks he is full of baloney and that her brother just never got over his "Twilight" obsession.)

All joking aside, my dad accidentally signed me up for Sports Camp, if you can believe that, which means that we actually have to DO the sports. (It's not as if it's five weeks of nothing but tailgate parties and in-the-stands spectatorhood.) Gopher said that I'll be "introduced" to many different sports in the hopes that I'll discover a hidden talent lying dormant for my entire life and just waiting to be revealed.

I hope that what she says is true — that I find my buried talent. I mean, out of a dozen or more sports to choose from, I have to find SOMETHING that I'm good at. Or if not "GOOD AT," then something that I can do marginally well and without landing me in the Intensive Care.

Oh! Before I forget... how cool is this?!! Girl Charlie is a super amazing gymnast from Texas, and she knows ... get ready for it ...

Simone Biles!!

("Knows" her in the sense that she's seen her across the room on the jungle gym or whatever and that wooden plank thingy she prances around on.) Do you want me to ask Charlie if she can get Simone's phone number for you? I can't make you any promises, but it won't hurt to ask.

That's all for now. Have a good summer and say HI to your sister for me.

Willa

July 23, 7:13 A.M.

Dear Dad,

OK. Now I'm worried since you haven't written or called me. Have you been abducted by aliens? (But I guess if you have, then you probably won't get this letter.)

The reason I mention the alien possibility is because one of the boys in the next cabin, Trenton (He's a fourth-year-er.) said that the year before last, the guys in his cabin saw a spaceship on Night Hike. (Night Hike is exactly what it sounds like. We have to hike in the dark — with flashlights, so it's a little less dangerous, but not much.) The spaceship didn't land, according to Trenton. I'm sure we would have heard about it on the news if it had. Trenton said it hovered overhead for about 10 seconds before it noiselessly swooshed across the sky like a comet. He also said it fouled the air with the putrid stench of rotten eggs and that it was so bad that the guys all started gagging. Later, they found out the smell wasn't from the spaceship. It had come from Darell. Dinner that night was meatloaf, and meatloaf gives Darell gnarly farts.

Please, please call or write! I NEED TO COME HOME!!!!

Love,

Willa

CAMP NEWS

July 23, 1:16 P.M.

Department of Child Social Services
United States of America

Dear Sir/Madam/Non-binary person,

I hope this letter finds you in good health. Unfortunately for me, if I cannot get your immediate assistance, I cannot say the same.

My name is Wilhelmina Eugenia Shisbey, and I am 13 years old. I am reaching out to you to seek help in rectifying a matter of upmost importance. I have been unsuccessful in reaching my father, Theodore Shisbey, DDS., of Huntington Beach, California. I cannot ascertain if he is intentionally avoiding my letters or if perhaps something untoward has happened to him. As I cannot reach him by post— the only method available to me since my electronic communication device was seized by the miscreants upon my incarceration (FYI, the device wasn't anything fancy, just an old iPhone that used to be my sister's with a cracked screen that made all my pictures look like a giant puzzle.), I had no other choice than to write to you.

I am currently being held against my will at Camp Mauch Chunk (a SPORTS CAMP!!), located in the Adirondack Mountains in northeastern Pennsylvania. To say I fear for my safety is an understatement! Are you aware that children at this camp are forced to sleep in tent-style structures? How can that possibly be safe? What if there's a tornado or a big gust of wind or something, or what if it rains and there's a tear in the canvas and the water pours in? Not only that, but we sleep in the middle of the forest where there's like wild animals and stuff! Did you know that bears apparently are just allowed to roam free? Isn't there some rule or ordinance or something where bears have to live in zoos?

And there are mosquitos EVERYWHERE —
hordes of them! It's common knowledge that
mosquitos can transmit malaria, dengue, West
Nile virus, chikungunya, yellow fever, filariasis,
tularemia, encephalitis, Ross River fever,
Barmah Forest fever, and the Zika virus, and as
we all know, a mosquito bite itches like nobody's
business!!

Additionally (and I insist on anonymity per the
"whistle-blower" status), I must inform you of
possible OSHA (Occupational Safety and
Health Administration) violations.

They include, but are not limited to, the
following:

1. There are 10 girls all CRAMMED inside a
   single cabin. (I think you need to check
   the maximum occupancy statute. Ten in a
   room seems like a lot to me.)

2. We have to sleep in bunkbeds! (I believe
   this breaks all "social distancing"
   regulations where I'm forced to breathe
   someone's used CO_2 and their stinky

morning breath for the next five weeks.)

3. There is only one bathroom. (Is that even legal — 10 girls sharing a single toilet?)

4. We have to walk to another building to TAKE A SHOWER! And the path is dirt with rocks and stuff on it, and you have to go up some rickety wooden stairs. Surely, that's a violation of the Americans With Disabilities Act? (Not that I've seen anyone in a wheelchair, but this IS a Sports Camp, so it's only a matter of time...)

5. How is it that Dodge Ball is still even LEGAL? Seriously, if there was ever a sport that breaks every "Wartime Rules of Engagement," it would be the hideous sport that is Dodge Ball.

Sincerely yours,

Wilhelmina (Willa) Shisbey

CAMP NEWS

July 25, 9:38 P.M.

Dear Dallas,

Please let Dakota and her attorney know (Is he your uncle? I noticed the last name is the same.) that I received the "**Cease and Desist**" letter and that I won't be writing Dakota again. Not to tell a lawyer how to do his business or anything, but did Dakota actually SHOW him my letter? I'm asking because the first "Charge," regarding **California Penal Code 523** has to do with **extortion** (which is when you threaten someone if they don't give you money), and I don't recall asking Dakota for anything. And the "Cyber" charge is totally bogus because the word cyber has to do with computer technology and the network it uses, and as we all know, my letter came by snail mail.

Thanks for writing!

Have a good summer and don't forget to use sunscreen.

Willa

P.S. Yes, I'll still try to get Simone's phone number for Dakota, and No, she doesn't have to pay me $5 for it.

CAMP NEWS

July 26, 9:32 A.M.

Department of Child Social Services
United States of America

Dear Director Steinheimer,

Please accept my deepest apologies for my earlier letter where I might have overstated my sense of peril here at Camp Mauch Chunk. It has been brought to my attention that in my heightened concern for my father (who is fine, by the way, and who made me write this letter or said I'd lose my allowance for the next five years) that I may have acted hastily in penning my concerns regarding my safety.

Kudos, however, to your "extraction team," for acting so quickly on my behalf! (If I ever really need to be saved, I'll know just who to call.) The SWAT team seemed quite efficient, and Gopher

— she's my cabin counselor — thought that a couple of the guys were "super hot." The battering ram might have been a bit much and ditto for the helicopter, especially since most of the structures here are tents and a good wind could knock them over (as evidenced by the total destruction of Wakanda, which will now be forced to rebuild).

In gratitude,

Willa Shisbey

CAMP NEWS

July 26, 9:40 P.M.

Dear Olivia,

Wow! I can't believe that you ACTUALLY wrote me back!

Gosh, in the world of technology with phones and computers, this has to be an Olivia Shisbey first — where you had to write to someone on a piece of paper (OK, so it looked a **teensy** bit like the burger wrapping from an In-N-Out cheeseburger — it was the logo and the big grease stain with the orange cheese stuck to the inside that gave it away), and using a … was that **lipstick** you wrote with? Or a red crayon maybe? But the fact that you took the time to write me, well, it came as a nice surprise. (FYI though, stamps can't be pulled off of other letters and reused even if it says it's a "Forever Stamp." Forever just means the value stays perpetual, not that you can reuse the same stamp "forever.")

I'm still in shock that you wrote me because I was sure that you hated me now that our family has been cleaved. (That means severed along a natural line.) NEVER in a million years did I expect to hear from you. Especially since you didn't speak to me when we lived in the same house, and that would have required far less effort than writing.

I'll answer your questions by going line by line. (And not to be a snarky know-it-all, but just in case you're studying for SATs or whatever and you want a little constructive advice, the first line of your letter should have read "Dear Willa," — D-E-A-R, and not "Deer Willa," like the animal.)

It might make it easier if I just rewrite your words and then give you my answers below your questions rather than giving them to you in story form. (I won't bother with spelling corrections. I mean, who wants to get a respond letter from someone like that. Right?? The fact you wrote to me, well, that's all that matters!)

1. Do U realy sleep in a tent?

Answer: Yes and no. The bottom half is made of wood, and the top is canvas. (That's the same fabric as my Converse shoes. But our canvas is army green, not black, like my shoes.) There is a wood frame that holds the canvas in place. So far, it seems waterproof. But I'll let you know if that changes.

2. Why duz your envelope say Camp Mauch Chunk? I thought Mom said you were at Camp Wannapee.

Answer: Camp Wanna Pee? Ha! Dad was kidding when he told her that. (Divorce can do strange things to adults. What is he, five?) There's a Camp "Tehachapi" across the lake. It sounds similar, but no, I can promise you, I am not at Camp Wannapee.

3. Do you have to yuz an outhouse to go #1 and #2? Also, do they have TP, or do you yuz leaves to wipe with?

Answer: Every cabin has a small bathroom inside with a sink and a regular toilet. (But the toilet paper is sort of thin and scratchy. I guess it's some special kind of paper that's used in RVs and is meant to dissolve quicker. The plumbing here is "sort of sketchy," according to the counselors, so it has to be biodegradable.) In case you're wondering, the showers are in a different building. And NO, the boys and the girls DO NOT use the same showers.

4. Where do you eat?

Answer: All the kids and counselors eat at the same time and in the same building referred to as the Grub Hub. (I think they stole the name from that food delivery service. You get a lot of copyright infringement up here... From the camp songs, to the names of our cabins and the different sports quadrants... I swear, I have yet to hear or see one creative thought! So far, it's just constant and flagrant plagiarism.)

5. Is swimming in the ocean there the same as our ocean here in Cali?

Answer: Ummm... To get to the Atlantic Ocean, I'd have to cross the state of New Jersey, which is east or to the "right" of Pennsylvania, if that makes it easier to understand. We do have a big lake we get to swim in, though, and it has a fun water slide and ropes and stuff. Plus, swim time is co-ed, and some of the boys are really cute, not to mention super coordinated — a requirement, I'm sure, since most are Junior Olympiads.

6. BTW, I still think it's all yur fault that our parents are getting divorced. Why did you have to be such a loser?

Answer: First of all, let me thank you for using the words "OUR PARENTS"!! Holy moly. You've never done that before. I sort of got used to the, "This is Willa. She's adopted ... as if you CAN'T TELL," introduction. And now you're adding me to the equation as an actual sibling?! THANKS SO MUCH!!

As to why I'm such a loser? ... I don't know... Genetics maybe? You gotta figure any mom who abandons their one-year-old kid at an orphanage in Chicago without leaving a forwarding address has to be one twist short of a Slinky, so maybe I get it from my biological mom.

Well, that's all for now. It's time for me to get

ready for our nightly campfire and storytelling.
(It's not as lame as it sounds, and the toasted
marshmallows are 'da bomb!)

Love,

Willa

P.S. Call or text Dad. He still can't figure out
why you're mad at him. He never wanted the
divorce.

CAMP NEWS

July 26, 9:51 P.M.

Dear Dallas,

Just to be clear, it's only Dakota who has the "Cease and Desist" against me, right? It wasn't some "Class Action" suit, was it? Because if that's the case, just rip up this letter and forget that I wrote you.

First off, Hi!

Are you having a fun summer so far? Have you been to the beach yet to watch Cody surf?

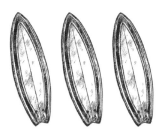

(And if so, is he as dreamy as ever?)

The reason that I'm writing you is because I need some "girly" help, and you and your sister are the girliest girls I know.

I guess I was supposed to bring stuff to decorate my individual bunk area, so I'm writing to you to get some suggestions. If you can, maybe call my dad and give him the list. He can buy the stuff and then send it to me. (FYI: Your sister has our house number. I know this because she kept making rude crank calls, not realizing that our landline has caller ID.)

Let me tell you some of the themes that my bunkmates have used, so you don't duplicate them.

The twins, Indy and Libby (and don't worry, you and Dakota are WAY way cuter than they are!), went with this "Hollywood Glam" thing. They have pink feather boas draped around their bed posts and white twinkly lights attached with hooks to the ceiling above their bunk. Their bedspreads are this metallic silver color and are topped with fuzzy white toss pillows. Libby's side of the wall has a framed picture of Marilyn Monroe, and Indy's side has a big white mirror where she's written her name with red lipstick.

Charlie's decor has this Hippie Chick/Boho Chic vibe. She has a tie-dyed sheet stapled to her wall and lots of mismatched pillows on her bed. There's a macramé hanging thingy (It just looks like a bunch of yarn on a stick to me.) above her bed (She has the top bunk.) and a couple of small baskets on top of her cubbies to hold her "personal items" (which is dumb, because obviously ANYTHING that belongs to her is a "personal item," not just the stuff inside the basket).

Amyfromatlanta (That's how she introduces herself, but it's actually AMY, and she's FROM Atlanta.) has her area decorated as an English

Rose Garden. She's stapled all of these plastic roses to the wall and spiraled fake ivy around the bedpost. (She has the bunk underneath me, and I had to prune her ivy because it was encroaching into my zone.) Her bedspread is really pretty, and it has pink and yellow flowers. She also had a bunch of potpourri (dead flowers and leaves basically) in a glass jar to "Infuse the cabin with the scent of spring!" but Gopher, our counselor, made her throw it out because it gave us all hay fever.

We also have a beach theme, a Moroccan bazaar, an Americana pseudo 4th of July thing, and a "Zen lounge."

Hopefully, that gives you an idea.

Thanks for your help!

Willa

CAMP NEWS

July 27, 1:59 P.M.

Dear Dad,

I received your "Care" package today. The cookies were delish! I shared them with my bunkmates. I admit, I'm trying to get them to like me, and as the saying goes, "The way to a ~~man's~~ GIRL'S heart is through ~~his~~ HER stomach!" Ha!

Hopefully, now I'll be able to sleep since you sent my pillow. So far, I haven't slept a wink, but my pillow might be the least of the problems. Last night, two bears were making such a racket that I had to zip my head inside my bubble jacket to try and drown out the noise. But come to find out — the noise wasn't coming from bears. It was from my cabin mates, Indy & Libby! They snore like you can't believe. Indy and Libby are twins and are swimming champs from Arizona. When I complained, Indy (Her real name is "Independence," and her sister's is "Liberty".) told me, "Suck it up, buttercup!" and that swimmers are big snorers and they can't help it. (Maybe water gets stuck in their nasal passages or something?)

And thanks for the 100 SPF sunscreen. FYI: Anything past 30 is a rip-off. There's only a two percent increase in protection from a 30 SPF to a 100. (It's misleading, I know, right?) My nose is already burnt, and I can tell that it's going to peel, which will be gross because sometimes those little dry pieces of skin hang underneath your nostrils and they look like boogers, and then all day everyone is staring at your nose and your booger look-alikes, except no one wants to say anything about it.

Sooo embarrassing!

Regarding the hat you sent... Not to sound ungrateful or anything, but I can't wear it. (Didn't you see the black Northface or the navy blue Volcom one on the top shelf of my closet?)

The pink HOTTIE hat was a "joke" hat. Sort of like the "Nice Underwear" front door mat and the bathroom "guestbook" that I gave you for Christmas where people are encouraged to "sign-in" when they use the toilet.

Olivia gave me the hat a year-and-a-half ago when she learned the definition of the word "Irony". (She pronounced it "I—Ronny".) Olivia thought it would be a hoot if I wore a hat that was the "TOTAL OPPOSITE" of me. Congrats, I guess, to Olivia who actually nailed the application of the word and extra points for attempting to put it into practice.

To answer your questions:

1. No! I AM NOT liking camp any better. (MY DEMAND STILL STANDS. PLEASE COME GET ME!!!!!!!)

2. Yes. I still cry at night. But thanks for sending Mister Snugglebum. I don't know how I'm going to hide a two-foot long stuffed rabbit, but I'll figure it out. Did he lose more stuffing? Now his left ear is drooping, too, and with both ears hanging down the sides of his head, he looks quite "forlorn.")

Please send me more goodies so I can move up the popularity chain quicker. (In a "JUST" world, one should not have to resort to bribery and snacks to be popular, but sadly that's not the case...)

Send:

Twizzlers (The red ones. Only grownups like licorice.)

Reese's Peanut Butter Cups (The minis.)

M & M's (No peanut. Amyfromatlanta is allergic.)

Pringles (Original, BBQ, Cheddar Cheese, Ranch, Sour Cream & Onion, and one can of Screamin' Dill Pickle for Suzy-Q. If you can't find it, it might be because it's a "seasonal flavor," in which case, she'll take Salt & Vinegar. But try to find the Screamin' Dill Pickle if possible because Suzy-Q has a a 3rd Degree Black Belt in Tae Kwon Do, and she scares me.)

Miss you tons,

XOXOXO

Willa

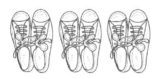

CAMP NEWS

July 27, 9:44 P.M.

Dear Cody,

I hope this letter finds you well. As for me ...
I'm well-ish.

I also hope you won't mind if I write to you
often. (And it's OK if you don't write me back.
I mean, it would mean A LOT to me if you DID
write me back, but if you DON'T want to write
me, well, I wouldn't be MAD or anything when I
see you next time, maybe just disappointed.)

One of the reasons for the letters is because
writing home to our families is sort of a
requirement. Maybe "requirement" is a stretch.
It's not as if we'll get kicked out if we don't write

home, or believe me, I'd never send a single letter in the hopes that they'd send me home on the first bus outta here!

The thing is, we work on a "points system" here at Camp Blow Chunks... I mean Camp Mauch Chunk.

If I had to guess, they got the point system idea from the U.S. Correctional Facilities Organization or something where the prisoners have to write home or they don't get that sliver of soap and 10-bristle toothbrush. But if our cabin wins the most points for letters home, we get to have an ICE CREAM party the Friday before camp ends. Whoo Hoo!

I know that technically you and I aren't "Family," at least, not blood related, but once I explained to the director that I DON'T HAVE A FAMILY ANYMORE on account of how my adoptive mom wanted to un-adopt me ... and how it caused this big hullabaloo (real word!) in the family, and how she ran off with Olivia, my adoptive sister — totally ditching my dad and me — and how now Diane and my dad are getting a divorce and it's all my fault because Diane never wanted me in the first place and only agreed to the adoption because they had seen the play "Annie" right before, and Diane thought that I'd be one of those cute singing and dancing orphan kids...

Whoa! Sorry. Talk about a run-on sentence!! (Ramble much, Willa??)

Enough of the retelling of my sad story. I'm sure you were sick of it the first, second, third, and twentieth time I called to tell you about it.

In summary: the director felt sorry for me once

I laid it all out and mustered up some crocodile tears for full effect. (I had to pinch myself to get them to flow, so I guess they weren't crocodile tears as much as they were tears of pain. Now I have a big bruise.) And so she encouraged me to write to whoever I wanted and that I'd still get "Family" points. Also, you might want to warn Carter, Conner, and probably your mom and dad, too, that they might be getting letters from me.

Oh, before I forget, the real reason I'm writing you is because I need to get some tips on how to burp. I mean, I know that if I drink a soda or something that I can eek out a little belch, but I need to know how to let one really rip. We're having a burping contest against the boys in The Dark Kingdom on Friday. Don't worry. There's nothing sinister going on up here. The Dark Kingdom is the name the boys chose for their cabin — it's a silly Disney thing. (Last year, the same cabin was named Snickerdoodle when they had to choose cabin names based on cookies.)

Catch ya later!

Willa

P.S. And if you could send me a few tips on how to whistle, that would be great, too. Apparently, we're supposed to whistle at night when we walk around camp to keep the bears away. I don't know if the kids are messing with me by saying that, but I don't intend to find out!!

Grrrr!

CAMP NEWS

July 28, 9:26 P.M.

Dear Dad,

I guess you heard, I did NOT have a heart attack this afternoon. (The nurse told me she called you. I guess she's required to call our parents when we're brought to "Sick Bay" on a stretcher. Some legal thing.)

I know I probably shouldn't question her diagnosis, but she's ONLY a NURSE, after all, not a doctor, so shouldn't she have gotten a "Second Opinion" or something? Because it sure FELT like a heart attack!

Apparently, I have a condition known as "Separation Anxiety." The nurse said it's common up here, and it's sometimes contagious. She told me that "TIME" is the cure. (And it strengthens my point that Camp Mauch Chunk needs to get a real doctor on staff ASAP. "Time" doesn't seem like something a doctor would prescribe. Wouldn't it be some sort of medicine?)

The nurse did give me something that is ALMOST as good as medicine, and that's milk and cookies. She said milk and cookies can cure almost anything.

I'll write you tomorrow and let you know if she's right.

Yours in anxiety,

Willa

July 29, 9:43 P.M.

Dear Marley,

Guess what?! Today I made a new friend. Her name is Luna Mooney. She might just become my camp BFF, but don't worry, no one will ever replace you!!!

I don't think I made a great first impression, though, because when Luna told me her name, I started laughing so hard that I choked on my spit.

I didn't laugh because I thought it's a strange name — I'm the LAST ONE to talk when it comes to weird names — I laughed because her full name is REDUNDANT. I don't have to tell

YOU, of ALL people, (Isn't your IQ score like 150?) that redundant is using two words together that mean the same thing, like "added bonus" or "early beginnings" or "final outcome." As you also probably know, LUNA is the Latin and Spanish word for moon, so her name is basically Moon Mooney.

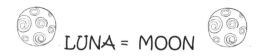

LUNA = MOON

Luna's not in my cabin, (although we're trying to hatch a plan to remedy that), and she is as awkward and dorky as I am. This is seriously a match made in nerdy girl heaven. She has this wispy blond hair that is sooo blond that it's almost white, big blue eyes, and a constellation of freckles on her face. And I'm not using "constellation" as a wordy over-exaggeration. I mean, once connected, her freckles literally come together as a recognizable star pattern.

Poor Luna still has the result of her "newbie hazing" on her face because her rotten cabin mates used a permanent marker to "connect-the-dots" while she slept. I didn't ask because she's still pretty sensitive about it, but I think the left side of her face is Ursa Major (the Little Dipper) and the right is Canis Major (Orion's Hunting Dogs, but it looks more like the stick figure guy in the paper and pencil game, "Hang Man"— only without the head — more than it looks like a dog.).

Luna's story is even sadder than mine. Her mom died a year ago. She didn't tell me how, and I didn't ask. Luna said her mom's greatest wish was for Luna to become a world class swimmer like her mom was as a teen. (I guess Luna was really good, too. She's won tons of medals and stuff, she said.) But ever since her mom died, Luna has refused to go back in the water, and her dad sent her here thinking that it might change her mind. But Luna said it was more likely that her dad sent her here so he could drink away the memory of her and her mother.

But on a funny note!

The boys in Pride Lands got in trouble today at breakfast, and you'll laugh when I tell you why. If I haven't mentioned it before, singing is a HUGE HUGE part of camp life. Seriously, it's like being stuck inside a bad music video most of the time. First, there's a main camp song. It's a total knockoff of the song, "We Are Family," by some group called Sister Sledge who's from my grandma's time (if I HAD a grandma), except instead of saying in the second line, "I got all my sisters with me," we sing it this way (and I'll write the words phonetically, so you can get the feel of it).

"WE are FAM-A-LEE! I got Mauch Chunkers with ME! We are FAM-A-LEE!! Get up everyBODY and SINNGGG!"

And then we also all have individual cabin songs. Ours is a take on the song, "Kumbaya My Lord." Amyfromatlanta came up with it. (She's a devout Christian and likes to say "Bless your heart" after she insults you to put a sweeter spin on it.) We had to take a vote on the song because several of the girls are from other faiths: Judaism, Muslim, and Hindu, but they thought it should be OK because it can be the "Lord" of their "understanding" and they can just insert the word of their personal deity if they want to.

Here's a little bit of the song. As you can see, we've inserted the name of our cabin to replace the word Kumbaya.

Arendelle, my Lord, Arendelle...

Arendelle, my Lord, Arendelle...

Arendelle, my Lord, Arendelle...

Ohhh, Lo…OOrdd, Are-en-delllle!"

Then we change the rest of the original words just a smidge, and instead of saying in the following stanzas that "someone's singing or crying or praying," like the real song says, we've changed it to "Someone's SWIMMING, my Lord," or they're VAULTING or JOUSTING, or whatever their sports deal is.

But back to the boys…

So the boys from the Pride Lands are all sitting together at their table at breakfast and using their Olympic athletic talents to see if they can accurately spit Cheerios across the table and into Payton's water glass. (I think his name is Payton. It might be Paxton.) Their counselor — Earthworm (I don't know why anyone would think Earthworm is a good Spirit Animal name. Is there ANYTHING lower on the evolutional ladder? Amoeba, maybe?), anyway, he starts singing the song, "Do Your Ears Hang Low?" It's a popular camp song that has a lot of different hand gestures that go along with it, simulating waving, rolling, tying, etc., and you do a different gesture with each new line. Then you repeat the song, and you go faster and faster each time, trying to keep up the momentum with the hand gestures until it's just a flurry of hand activity.

The song goes like this:

Do your ears hang low?

Do they wobble to and fro?

Can you tie them in a knot?

Can you tie them in a bow?

Can you throw them o'er your shoulder

like a Continental soldier?

...

Do your ears hang low?

ONLY... Ethan (or maybe it's Evan. Seriously, I've met so many kids it's hard to keep them straight!) decides to change one little word, just one, and it results in total chaos!

Mar! He changed the word "ears" to the word "boobs!"

Just picture over a 100 kids flailing their arms while singing at the top of their healthy athletic lungs about hanging, wobbly, knotted, and bow-tied mammaries.

Pride Lands got a bunch of demerits since they were the "instigators" of the chaos, and as a punishment, they now have bathroom cleanup for a week.

That's all for now. I'll write again soon!

Love,

Willa

P.S. Yes, I still hate camp. But I hate it a little less.

CAMP NEWS

July 30, 9:27 P.M.

Dear Dallas,

You can tell your sister that I'm on to her dirty tricks.

I get the joke — giving my dad a list of Harry Potter paraphernalia to decorate my bunk. Because, SURE! How would my poor unsuspecting dad know that NO WAY, NO HOW would I EVER decorate my space with all things HARRY POTTER! (Not anymore at least. When I was six, maybe.)

But the real stab to the heart was that you and your sister had him send me...

SLYTHERIN!!!!

DO I LOOK LIKE I'D BE FROM SLYTHERIN??

Gryffindor would be a stretch — I'll grant you that. Brave and daring, I'm not. And even Hufflepuff is a reach, what with all of their "patience and loyalty." But what about Ravenclaw? Witty and Intelligent. Ravenclaw would have my name all over it!

I am SO **NOT** going to string up those cheesy green plastic LED lights with the black snakes. And the Hogwarts' "Slytherin Pride" poster is going right back into the box. Ditto for the green and black wall shield with that horrifying coiled viper. The "I'm a Proud Slytherin" bedspread (as comfy as it looks) is also going back in the box.

But I'm keeping the green socks and only because wearing socks with snakes on them might actually help me repel real snakes, and I need as much help as I can get because snakes are a big issue up here, AND...

In case you don't know...

I AM DEATHLY AFRAID OF SNAKES!!!!!!!

(So tell your sister I said, Thanks but No thanks!)

Willa

August 1, 1:36 P.M.

Dear Dad,

Please send the following:

1) OFF

2) DEET

3) REPEL

4) Or... 50 rolls of toilet paper that I can wrap myself in to keep the mosquitoes from biting me. I now have more mosquito bites than I have zits, and as you know, that's quite a bit.

5) RID (Rid is for a different kind of bug. It's lice killer. I don't have lice. YET. But it's going around camp, and I want to be prepared.)

6) Another gigantic container of red licorice. (I only got one measly piece after the vultures in my cabin got ahold of the last container.)

7) 10 bags of Doritos. Assorted flavors. And not the mini bags, but the full-sized jumbo ones. (No, they are not all for me. I'll give a bag to each of my bunkies.)

8) More flashlight batteries.

9) So, this one is kind of embarrassing, but I need a week's worth of underwear. (Mine keep getting stolen.) And FYI, by "week's worth," I mean the kind of underwear with the days of the week printed on them. (This is a "Don't Ask, Don't Tell," so don't ask.) To get the proper size and brand, grab one from the stack of Sunday in my drawer. Please do not disturb the other days of the week.

Monday Tuesday Wednesday Thursday Friday Saturday

But please go to the store and buy me a new

pack because if people are going to steal my underwear, I don't want them stealing stained ones.)

Thank you. I love you!

Willa-bo-billa

CAMP NEWS

August 1, 9:33 P.M.

Dear Connor,

Thanks so much for writing to me and giving me the burping tips, but I don't believe for a minute that Cody is now "too old and sophisticated for such uncouth behavior, such as burping," as you put it, so that's why you're writing me instead of him. (Besides, aren't you only in FOURTH grade? Those are some pretty big words for a fourth grader. They're even big words for Cody. HA! So tell your brother that I know he told you to say them and how I said I think he's using big words to show off.)

I want to review these burping tips with you before I try them. I told my new camp BFF, Luna, that I was going to sign up for the Burping Contest, and she said I better make sure to practice so that the air comes out of my

93

MOUTH during the contest and not the bottom half of me! (Ha!)

1. <u>The Air Gulp</u>: You say to make sure that I do a big EXHALE first. Then I just keep SWALLOWING air as if I'm EATING it? Is that right? And then I'm supposed to clench my stomach muscles like I'm holding in the urge to … well, YOU know what you said … before letting it out in one long noisy burp? OK. So far that one seems doable.

2.<u>The Fizzy Chug</u>: We don't have Slurpees up here, like you suggested, but I should be able to get my hands on a soda. (Does it matter what flavor?) For that one, you say I'm supposed to chug the can down as quickly as possible and then when I feel the rumbling in my stomach that I'm supposed to lean FORWARD. Why forward? Is that in case the soda makes me want to hurl and it gives me a clear shot to the floor, or does it maybe project the burp sound or something? It seems to me that it would make more sense to lean backwards to project the sound, but then you're the expert.

3. <u>The Reverse Sip</u>: I totally DON'T get what you're saying on this one. I'm supposed to drink a glass of water from the OPPOSITE side of the glass??? How is that even possible? Doesn't the water just dump all over the front of my face? Is Cody punking me on that one??

Well, thanks again for taking the time to write back to me! Wish me luck!

Willa

P.S. Please tell Cody that No, I don't want to know how to do a "Loon Call" whistle (whatever that is), just a regular one.

P.P.S. Has anyone ever told you that for a boy, you have really pretty writing?

So pretty...

August 2, 9:43 P.M.

Dear Dad,

I got your letter. Thanks for all of the treats. They must be helping with my "street cred" because my bed has only been short-sheeted once this week. As I'm sure you know, short-sheeting is an annoying prank where someone folds your sheets in half like an envelope so you can't put your legs straight. (Only you DON'T KNOW that's the problem, so you look like a total nitwit while you struggle to push your legs inside your sheets and everyone laughs like it's the funniest darn thing they've seen in their entire life!)

But the purpose of this letter is to clarify something you said.

WHAT DO YOU MEAN THAT YOU CAN'T COME TO PARENTS' WEEKEND????

It's YOUR weekend! That's why they name it "PARENTS' WEEKEND."

I don't want to be a big crybaby, but I can't help it. It's just that I miss you so so so so MUCH! And I'm trying to be a "tough cookie" like you say, but I miss you, and my bed, and Marley, and Cody, and Sam, and Robbie... and even that mean neighbor, Old Lady Pearson, who yells at me to stay off her lawn.

I guess I'm not a tough cookie after all. I'm a soggy one. And I need to see you!

I just don't fit in up here, Dad. (Not that I fit in all that great back home, but at least I have a few friends who don't think I'm a TOTAL loser.) I've tried almost every sport in the rotations, and so far, I'm HOPELESS at EVERYTHING! I'm not kidding!

I'm too short for basketball.

Too uncoordinated for volleyball.

Too slow for … well, pretty much EVERYTHING!!! You name it. I'm too slow for it:

Soccer LaCrosse, Field Hockey, Competitive Swimming…

And I'm downright "untrainable" (according to the instructors) in gymnastics and martial arts. The only thing I haven't tried is archery, and that's only because the director wants to "up" the camp's liability insurance before they hand me something as dangerous as a bow and arrow.

I don't care if you have "DENTAL OBLIGATIONS," as you put it, and have "EXTRACTIONS" the Friday before. Can't the girl who answers the phone do them? How hard can it be to pull someone's teeth out? They pretty much just fall out on their own when you're a kid.

Please reconsider!!!!

Yours in despair,

Willa

CAMP NEWS

August 3, 7:39 A.M.

TO: The Occupants of Arendelle

FROM: Willa Shisbey

RE: My Underwear (Again!)

Dear Bunkmates,

Seriously! What is your DEAL with underwear???

I am now missing my SATURDAY and SUNDAY! I know how much everybody loves the "weekend," but come on, guys, there's no way I can substitute my weekdays for the weekend.

PLEASE RETURN... (No questions asked.)

Willa

CAMP NEWS

August 4, 9:42 P.M.

Dear Marley,

Have you ever thought to yourself about how GREAT it would be to get woken up every morning at 7:30 A.M. to the recorded bugle sounds of "Reveille"?

No? Me neither.

Because IT IS AWFUL!!!!!!!!! Seriously, no wonder the military can't get anyone to join. One week of having to listen to THAT every morning, and it would be "sayonara" and "adios." (Plus, the dumb song gets lodged in your brain, so all day long, you hear: Da-da-dada-Dah. Da-da-dada-Dah. Da-da-dada-Dah DA—DA-DAH! Da-da-

dada-Dah! Da-da-dada-Dah! Da-da-dada—DA-DA-DA! Da-da-da-da-da-**DAH-DA!** Da-da-da-da-da-**DA!** Da-da-da-da-da-**DAH-DA!** Da-da-da-da-da-**DAH!**...

I told you that I would send you my daily activity schedule, so here it is:

7:30 A.M. —REVEILLE: Time to rise and shine for another miserable day.

8:00 A.M. — LINE UP: We have to stand in line while they raise the flag and make announcements. (It's even worse than school.)

8:15 A.M. —BREAKFAST: It's buffet style, and we sit together as a "family" with our counselor and bunkmates. (The food is actually pretty good.)

9:30 A.M. — CLEAN UP: We return to our cabins to clean. The cabin with the highest score for the week wins a surprise. (I'm now responsible for making EVERYONE'S beds since I'm the only one who apparently knows HOW TO

MAKE A BED, and we really really want to win.)

9:45-10:45 A.M. — PERIOD 1: "Land" activities that may include but are not limited to: soccer, basketball, tennis, martial arts, gymnastics, archery, Quidditch... (Ha! Just seeing if you're on your toes because OBVIOUSLY Quidditch would be considered an "aerial" sport.)

11:00 A.M.-12:00 P.M. — PERIOD 2: Water activities that may include swimming and boating or, if you're me, hiding in the bushes so nobody sees me in my bathing suit.

12:30 P.M. — LUNCH: Pizza! Tacos! Burgers! Falafels! (Not a fan, BTW. Have you tried them? They're shaped like meatballs but made with beans instead of meat.)

1:15-2:10 P.M. —REST HOUR: (I don't know why it's called Rest **"Hour"** because it's only 55 **minutes.**) We don't really rest — except for Gopher, who closes her eyes and PRETENDS that she's not listening to everything we say —

instead, we're in our cabin reading our mail or refolding the clothes in our cubbies. (At least, that's what I do during rest hour. Everyone else has fun playing board games with one another and bragging about how fabulous they are.)

2:15 P.M. SNACK — It's milk and cookies. Is it me, or does milk and cookies following Rest Hour remind you of what happens in kindergarten?

2:20-3:05 P.M. — HOBBY PERIOD: It's "Camper Choice" so we can go to any activity that we want. The Olympiads usually spend it at their specialized sport. So far, I haven't found anything that I'm good at, but I've yet to try Archery or Trapeze.

3:15-4:15 P.M. — PERIOD 4: Bunk Activity. We vote on something to do as a group, but because it's "majority wins," it's usually a GRASS SPORT since there are more of those girls in my cabin. Charlie works on her "floor exercise" and does her gymnastic tumbling routine while she's on the field, and Suzy-Q does her Ninja stuff. Indy and Libby usually get permission to go to the pool. That pretty much leaves me to be "ball catcher." Today, I almost got attacked by wasps when the soccer ball disturbed a wasp nest hidden inside a bush. Amyfromatlanta said that with how fast I was running, maybe track and field is my hidden talent.

4:30-5:30 P.M. — PERIOD 5: "Free Choice." (I don't know why they just don't call it "Camper Choice: Part 2" because it's pretty much the same thing except it's at the lake.) We can swim, go sailing, waterskiing, paddle boarding, or fishing. Of course, it's assuming one knows how to do those things in the FIRST PLACE, which, of course, I don't. Except for swimming. I know how to swim. (But you know what's funny? Not ha-ha funny, but odd. I can't convince Luna to go in the water with me. She's supposed to be some great swimmer, but she refuses to go. What do you think that's all about?? I hope I can convince her because so far she's the only friend

I've made, and it's lonely being in a lake all by myself.)

5:30-6:00 P.M. — SHOWER TIME: Every day before dinner. (A shower is mandatory. I guess it's important for boys to know that.)

6:00 P.M. — LINE UP: The flag is lowered, and then the senior counselors do a "Shout Out" over the loudspeakers of highlights and accomplishments of some of the most noteworthy campers of the day.

6:15 P.M. — DINNER: Buffet style with main dish choices, like lasagna, chicken stir-fry, or tasteless and gross vegan stuff.

6:45-7:30 P.M. — TRIBE TIME: It's pretty much camp anarchy where we get to run around and blow off steam, or for the more mellow campers, hang out in groups and listen to the campers who brought their guitars. I usually hang out with Luna, and we commiserate and whine about how much we miss home.

7:40-9:00 P.M. — EVENING ACTIVITY: I have to say, this is my favorite part so far. Last night, we watched the boys have a belly flop contest off the dock, which was really fun (although it made me miss Cody). The night before that we had a campfire and got to have s'mores. It almost seemed like a movie, Mar, with the fire glowing and the frogs burping in the distance while the fireflies bounced around in the dark like tiny sparklers. We're going to do a team "Zombie Scavenger Hunt" (whatever that means) on one of the nights, and the last week of camp, there's a talent show. Not sure if I'm up for that!

9:15 P.M. — TAPS: Thankfully, it's not the funeral song, "Taps." (That thing is depressing.) Instead, we all gather in our individual cabin groups, and we sing our camp Alma Mater, "We Are Family" (which is quite peppy), while dancing our way to our cabins. (Watching the boys sashay and get all funky monkey is really funny!)

10:00 P.M. — LIGHTS OUT: And thank goodness. Because after a day of all that physical stuff, this kid is too pooped to pop!

So now you'll know where I'm at during the different times of the day. Please send me good vibes or juju or whatever when you see that I'm having "sports time." I need all the help I can get!

Love you,

Willa

August 9, 9:43 P.M.

Dear Mrs. A,

Thank you SO MUCH for coming to Parents' Weekend as my unofficial "Parent!" Can I KEEP you pretty please?!!! I would love to have Marley as my sister! (But we'd have to find a way to square things with Mr. A and my dad. Alternating months, maybe? HA!)

What a coincidence that you had to come east for the doctor's oncology convention or talk or whatever it was that you had to do in New York after I saw you. Is there much advancement yet in the treatment for kids with cancer? I sure hope so!!

wish hope

Please send me copies of the selfies and pictures. You'll have to print them and mail them to me, though, because I'm stuck in a time bubble from 1972 where we aren't allowed anything to be sent digitally. You don't need to include the ones you took of me falling out of the canoe or being rescued from the Rock Wall. (I still say my harness malfunctioned!) So maybe just send me the ones where we're making the tie dye T-shirts or where we're sitting together around the campfire with the other Arendelle "family members."

Besides wanting to thank you for coming, I'm writing because I wanted to ask you something while you were here, but I was too embarrassed, so I'll ask you now. Since you're a doctor, you can give me your professional opinion.

Remember that "odd-looking flag," I believe is how you phrased it, that you pointed out flying on the top of my cabin? (If I remember correctly, you also added the word "ratty.") Well, in full disclosure, it wasn't a flag. It was my bra. The boys from Mount Olympus staged a "panty raid" on our cabin the first week of camp, and my bra was part of their "Pirate's Booty" (which, of course, you know means a pirate's TREASURE, not a pirate's BUTT). As far as bras go, the boys said it was their most disappointing one yet. (Thank goodness I never got around to writing my name inside all of my clothes like I was supposed to, or they would have known it belonged to me!!)

I heard their disappointment wasn't so much from the rattiness of it as it was the small cup size. So my question to you is, as a 13-year-old, when should I expect a "growth spurt" in that area? Shouldn't things be moving along by now? Is there some formula or ratio I can use that corresponds with my shoe size or height or something to forecast where I might be headed?

Well, that's all for now. Again, thank you, thank you, thank you for coming to see me. You have no idea HOW HAPPY it made me!! Please tell Marley that I miss her tons (and that I want to steal her mom from her!).

With love and appreciation,

Willa

August 9, 9:51 P.M.

Dear Marley,

Thank you so much for coming up with the idea that your mom should come and be my "Weekend Mom" before she headed to her doctor's convention in New York. I have to admit, I cried just a teensy bit when I went to bed the first night after she arrived when all of the girls in my cabin were sitting around and bragging about how great their moms are and all of the hardships that their moms go through in order to support their daughters in their athletic endeavors. I even had one crazy moment where I wanted to shout at all of them, "GET REAL!!!

YOUR MOMS ARE ONLY IN IT FOR THE GLORY!!!!"

It made me think how life is so unfair and how almost everyone at camp has these great moms who are such a big part of their kid's life while I've now had two moms bail out on me. My birth mom — and now Diane, (Do you see a trend here?) and both within the first 14.444 percent of my life (assuming I can make it to age 90).

I was commiserating with Luna, the only other momless camper here, and she said a couple of really profound things regarding our difficult lives. (This stuff is super deep, so there's a strong chance she's quoting Yoda.)

Luna said this:

1.) "Not everything that's broken can be fixed."

And 2.) ...

"Sometimes you're the windshield, sometimes you're the bug."

Profound, right?

Well, that's about all for now. We're getting ready to play the game, "**Two Truths and a Lie.**" Have you ever played it before? I've never known you to lie, so my guess is No.

But in case you want to know, here's how you play it:

Everyone sits in a circle, and each person takes a turn telling the group three things about themselves: two that are true and one that's a lie. The group then discusses the choices out loud, and they have to agree on which one they think is the lie. Then you tell them if they guessed correctly. I'm really gonna stump 'em! Because one of my truths will be that I have H-

SAM and that I can remember every day of my life with computer accuracy (as you know!), and my other truth will be that I had a collection of over 12,000 novelty erasers. I think my lie will be that I'm good in math. (Why is it that everyone assumes I'm good at math? My black-framed glasses maybe??)

Write back!!

Love,

Willa

CAMP NEWS

August 11, 1:17 P.M.

Dear Cody,

OH, MY GOSH! YOU ARE NOT GOING TO BELIEVE THIS!

I'm GOOD at SOMETHING!

REALLY GOOD, IN FACT.

I'm not a total uncoordinated goof like I originally thought.

I'VE FINALLY DISCOVERED A SPORT WHERE I ROCK!!

I was almost ready to give up hope that I'd be good at ANYTHING because I'd tried one sport after the other and each was more hazardous

117

than the next. (Either to me—or my teammates.)

Competitive swimming was a total joke. Like, literally the other girls had completed their laps in the pool and were already in the showers, and I was still butterflying my way across the shallow end like a Monarch with only one wing and drowning in molasses.

You've said yourself how out of shape I am when it comes to running, so it will come as no surprise that any sport involving a repetitive forward movement of my legs was a NO GO. (Cross off Field Hockey, Soccer, and Track and Field ... check... check, double check.)

I'm too short and weak-armed for Basketball and Volleyball. (But I seemed to have a spot-on aim in volleyball when it involves the back of Emma's head.)

And take a guess at how well I did at Gymnastics! …

HORRIBLE!! Although the coach DID tell me that I excelled at TUMBLING. (She didn't mean to suggest I was good at flips, handsprings, and somersaults. She meant that I excelled at tumbling OFF of the gym equipment. Have you ever fallen off a "horse?" I don't recommend it.)

In a million years, you will never guess what sport I'm good at. (Part of the reason you won't be able to guess is because if you're like me, you probably didn't know that it's even considered a "sport.")

Are you ready to hear? Are you REALLY REALLY READY?

IT'S ARCHERY!!!!

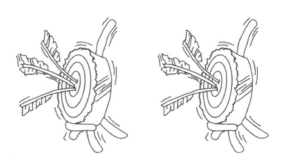

Yes. Archery. As in, USING A BOW AND ARROW! Only it's not the old-fashioned kind like in the Cowboy and Indian movies. This is Olympic-style archery using something called a RECURVE BOW. (A recurve bow bends AWAY from the archer. Ours are made out of fiberglass.)

In case you don't know much about archery (and let me tell you, what you see in the movies is a total crock!), here are five Basics that are important if one wants to become a good "Archer."

1. Pick a bow that fits you. The bow has to be the right size for your height and the right draw (pull) weight for your ability.

2. Proper stance. Your feet need to be in the same place every time, and your lower body supports your upper body, which does all the work. There are a couple of different stances, but I won't bore you with the details right now. (Instead, I can bore you in person when I show you them the next time I see you.) It's important to be consistent and stand the same way for every shot.

3. Align your upper body. It's important to have your shoulders in a straight line to allow your bone structure to support the weight of the bow.

4. Find a good anchor point. This is probably the most important thing. The anchor point is the place that your "draw hand" rests when it draws the bowstring back to your face. Again, consistency is the key!

5. Smoothly release the arrow. (Cody, it is the COOLEST feeling!!) It's a little tricky because you have to do a "clean" release where you

minimize the back-and-forth movement of the bowstring just before each shot. Then you maintain eye focus, keeping your eye on the target, not the arrow, and BAM!

BULLSEYE, BABY!!!!

Here's the deal! Do you want to know WHY I'm so good at it? And it's the darndest thing! Cody, I'm so good at archery because of my H-SAM!!!

Yes, my horrible, awful, freakazoid problem where every single day of my life is as equally vivid in my memory as the last. I never thought H-SAM would be a "good thing," having all of my memories stored forever in my brain and all the way back to the day my mom left me at the orphanage as a baby. But with my ability to recall almost every moment of my life by mentally scrolling through a daily "timeline," all I have to do is close my eyes and recall the moment of the LAST bullseye. In real time, I can then remember where my feet were placed and the height I held the bow. I know the perfect amount of tension I used and the exact anchor point I focused on. Each and every time will be a perfect DUPLICATION of the last!

IT WORKS, CODY!

Once I made the first bullseye (The coach was so excited he almost wet his pants — everyone had pretty much given up on me by then.), all I had to do was bring back the memory and duplicate it. Again. And Again. And Again.

I HIT 10 BULLSEYES IN A ROW!!

I'M A PHENOM!!! (I'm sure, as you know, a "phenom" is someone with phenomenal ability or talent.) Coach said he's even going to name my signature move, "The Willa." (It's where you have to scrunch up your face and bite your lip before your release your arrow.)

I am so happy that I could cry and actually did — like a total baby — when they announced my name over the loudspeaker at evening Lineup. The counselors said I'm now the camp record holder for consistent bullseyes, and that according to Coach, I might even have a real shot at the Olympics in the future. The OLYMPICS, Cody!! How cool is that! After they announced it, tons of kids came over to me and were high-fiving and hugging me and stuff, and a few even asked if they could have my autograph! I'm sure they were teasing, and I didn't have a paper or pen on me, but in case they weren't, I've made some signed copies that I'll keep in my pocket to give them the next time they ask.

I just CANNOT believe that I'm now a JOCK! Cody and Willa, both jocks. Who would have ever thought it? Sadly, I won't get to show off my mad sports skills at school. Not unless I can convince the school board to add Archery to the electives, but with all of the recent budget cuts, I don't see that happening anytime soon.

Well, that's all for now.

XOXOXO,

Willa, AKA, Katniss Everdeen

Camp News

August 12, 9:35 P.M.

Dear Dad,

Be afraid. Be very afraid...

HA! Just kidding. But now that I have your undivided attention, GUESS WHAT!!!

You are now looking (Well, you're not LITERALLY "looking" — obviously... since you're more than 2000 miles away from me, but you get my drift.) at a future Olympic gold medalist in... (drumroll, please ... Dah... Dah... Da... Daaah...!! ARCHERY!!!

Yes, Dad — Archery. The bow and arrow stuff of legends and Robin Hood, and in more recent times, "The Hunger Games."

It just so happens that I have "real talent," according to my coaches. Like, "This kind of talent only comes along once every 20 years" talent.

Can you believe it?

The only explanation I can come up with is that it must tie in with my H-SAM. Come to find out, H-SAM has a positive use besides being able to recall what the weather was on any given day in the past 12 years or recall that you've yelled at me on three separate occasions since you adopted me.

The specific days were: Sunday, April 4, the first year I lived with you. Remember how I got a pink Peep stuck up my nose (Those things are super squishy!) on Easter Sunday, and you had to take me to Urgent Care to get it removed?

Or on July 4th, the year I was eight, when I set the patio table on fire (along with all of the food) when my sparkler caught the end of the red white and blue paper tablecloth? Holy smokes, were you mad (but not nearly as mad as Diane!) when the fire department had to come and on such a busy day for them.

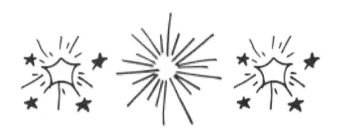

And I can VIVIDLY REMEMBER September 22, the year I was nine, when you attempted that midnight raid on the refrigerator and stepped on my Lego that I'd left on the kitchen floor. I think you even managed to wake up the neighbors with all of your yelling. (Although why you couldn't have waited till morning to yell at me, I don't know.)

But that stuff is all in the past because now for the first time I have people admiring me! Even stopping me when they see me in camp to give me a high five or to compliment me.

YIPPEE!!

I am SO happy!!!

Between practically bribing my bunkmates to like me with all of the cool snacks you've been sending (thanks again, BTW) and now with my newfound talent, I'm moving up from everyone's label of me as: "That nerdy girl, Willa-what's-her-face." to "That nerdy girl, Willa-what's-her-face with the MAD bow skills."

THINGS ARE DEFINITELY LOOKING UP FOR THIS KID!!

Love,

Willa

P.S. OK, I have to come clean. I am starting to like camp.

August 14, 9:50 P.M.

Dear Marley,

Oh, my goodness. Where to start?!

First off, I'm now officially an "Archer."

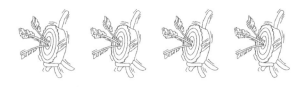

Seriously!

I know it sounds a bit "rugged" for someone with my lack of physical strength and coordination, but come to find out, I'm a natural at it. I'll go into more detail later or, better yet, I'll show you my skills when I come home and slice an apple in half from the top of Dakota's head at 50 paces. (I'm quite accurate, but I'd feel better if I tried it with Dakota rather than someone I care for.)

But the reason I'm writing is... remember Luna, my camp BFF? And how I told you that for some reason she wouldn't go in the water even though she had been a competitive swimmer? Instead, when it's "lake time," she's either the towel monitor or the raft blower-upper. Well, last night when Luna and I walked back to our cabins, I shared how my birth mom ditched me and left me at an orphanage when I was a baby because of my cleft lip and messed-up face. I explained how I had to live in the orphanage for years until my dad adopted me cuz he felt sorry that no one else wanted me. How he'd come to work on our teeth as the visiting dentist and how every year I'd still be there, even though all of the other kids had been adopted.

Luna felt super sorry for me. (I'd forgotten that the story can be a real "tear jerker.") And she then shared with me her secret — why she won't go near the water.

Mar, it's so sad... It's because her mom drowned.

Luna said the family was on vacation in Florida, and her mom was swimming in the ocean. The water had been pretty choppy that day because it was hurricane season or something, and there was a terrible rip current. Her mom was a super strong swimmer in pools, but I guess the current was too much for her, and it swept her out beyond the break.

Luna was on the beach when the lifeguards brought her mom's body back to shore, but by then, her mom had passed. The whole thing is quite tragic and reminds me how lucky I am, despite all of my whining to the contrary.

But here's the good news! And depending on if you want to see the glass as half-empty or half-full, I'm either to be blamed or thanked for getting Luna back into the water where she belongs!! (Honestly, Mar, Luna is crazy-good at swimming!!)

During Free Choice, I went to the lake and decided that I'd have a relaxing float in one of the tube rafts. Luna was working the raft shack, and she gave me the oversized one that I like. I thought I heard a slight sssssss, when she gave it to me, like it had a leak, but the trees sort of make that same sound when the wind blows through them, so I didn't think too much about it. Most of the other kids were jumping off the end of the dock or coming down the water slide, but I found a nice little spot where I could just float along in my raft and revel in my new success at being good at SOMETHING for the first time in my life.

I must have dozed off for a couple of minutes because the next thing I knew my raft had completely collapsed, and I was submerged in the water! Thoughts of Luna's mom flashed through my mind, and I totally panicked started splashing around screaming HELP! HELP! The lifeguard was too busy flirting with that cute counselor — Otter — to notice me, but Luna did! She saw me thrashing and yelling, and she hightailed it down the beach and into the water. She swam like there's no tomorrow to save me!

And save me she did — from a depth of three-and-a-half feet of water. I guess when I fell asleep, I still hadn't made it out of the shallow part, so there was less chance of me drowning than maybe getting the runs from gulping lake water.

But even more importantly, it cured Luna's fear of the water! Once Luna dragged me on shore with that one-arm-under-the-boob thing that lifeguards do, she realized what she did and how she'd managed to face her fears, and she got up on the dock and made a spectacular dive into the water to swim out to fetch my sunken raft. A kid named Chase dove in after her, and the race was on! Luna totally outswam him by half a length. (At least, I think that's the terminology unless it's supposed to refer to the entire "length" of the lake, which wasn't the case.)

Everybody cheered for Luna, and now the two camp nerds, Luna and yours truly, are all everyone is talking about. And not because Luna and I have funny names or because Luna has as many freckles as the stars in the sky, or I have glasses or a scar where my cleft used to be, but because at Camp Mauch Chunk (a place for "Fostering Athletic Excellence!"), we've now earned our right to be here — just as much as anyone else.

Oh, I gotta go! We're having a meeting about the upcoming talent show. I'm not sure yet what I'll do, but as they say, THE SKY IS THE LIMIT!

Love,

Wills

P.S. Camp is a blast!

August 15, 9:32 P.M.

Dear Cody,

I LOVE camp!

Looking back, I can't believe that I was such a big baby. Wahhh!

New friends. New experience. And the GREAT OUTDOORS! What's not to like? (And NO, the real Willa has not been abducted by aliens and replaced with the girl writing you this letter.)

From here on out, I'm going to INSIST that my dad send me to camp every single year — or until he goes totally broke and can't afford it any longer.

I guess I'll just have to get a babysitting job (bleh!) and save up money, so I can pay my own way in case the divorce puts him financially in the toilet. What's the hourly rate these days for a babysitter? Do you know? I'll have to do some serious number crunching because I think camp is thousands of dollars, and that's going to require A LOT of babysitting! I'll have to expand to dog walking if the babysitting alone doesn't cut it. People are willing to pay a lot more money for the care of their pets than for their kids from what I hear.

Since this is the last full week of camp, we had our big talent show last night. Sounds super cheesy. Right? That's EXACTLY what I thought when I heard about it. I had visions of bad lip-synching and cheerleading. Or worse, INTERPRETIVE dance! (I SO don't get the deal with all that twirling and flouncing and rolling around on the floor. It's not interpretive of anything I've ever seen. Fairies frolicking in a field maybe? Or dogs rolling in grass?)

At first, I was super stressed because I couldn't come up with a "talent." I asked if I could cut the overhead lights and have the room go dark and show off my mad archer skills by lighting my arrows on fire and shooting at targets onstage, but that was a big N to the O. So I had to think think think.

What skill did I possess that might entertain? And you know what I came up with? (But first, promise not to laugh because I've kept this "talent" of mine a secret, and even Marley doesn't know about it.)

Cody, I can Yo the Yo out of a yoyo.

Yoyo, baby!

I'd sorta forgotten about my yoyo talent. Especially because yoyos bring back bad memories of my time in the orphanage. The Christmas when I was three and the other kids were scattering Christmas paper, unwrapping their Santa gift of a doll, or a toy train, or a stuffed animal, I sat alone in a corner and unwrapped my tiny single gift. A yoyo. (And not even a nice quality one, but the 99-cent kind.)

I played with the yoyo as much as I could until the string broke, which was soon after. I remember the day after it broke, my dad (This was before he adopted me and was just the dentist who came for our cleanings.) found me crying in the corner over my broken yoyo. He tried to fix the string with some dental floss, but it was the waxy kind and didn't work. The next day, he returned with a Duncan. I still have that first yoyo he bought me, but over the years, I expanded my talent. Now I have a couple of high-tech ones.

I was the last "ACT" in the lineup, which is always a concern, because then you have all of the other acts to compare. And I gotta say, some of the other acts were pretty darn good. The guys in Sugar Rush did a boy-band, K-pop thing, and the girls LOVED IT!! They screamed and pretend cried. Not that the guys from Sugar Rush sounded very good, but they sure looked the part in their black suits and white shirts.

The girls in Pixie Hollow (Most of who are gymnasts.) did a Cirque du Soleil act, and the boys LOVED IT!! They screamed and pretend cried. (Because what boy doesn't want to see cute girls in leotards and doing the splits in mid-air?)

There was a Sit-Down Stand-Up comedy act by a couple of the guys in Wakanda. (They called it Sit-Down Stand-Up because one guy was the "dummy" and he was sitting down and the ventriloquist guy stood up behind him.) That act was only so-so. Lamar's lips were moving the whole time.

There were a few singers, some with guitars, and one act where a girl from Narnia played an "Oboe." (And I only use quotes because I was corrected when I called it a clarinet.)

Some of the girls in my cabin did this cool hand-clapping routine to the song, "We Will Rock You," by Queen. They got a standing ovation, and it was well deserved.

My friend Luna got super creative, and she built this underwater backdrop. Dressed as a mermaid, she sang the song, "Under the Sea," while suspended from overhead ropes and "swimming" across the stage.

Like I said, I went last, and when it was my turn (and after I dry-heaved into the trashcan next to the stage from nervousness), I prepared the stage with a solid black backdrop — my clothes were black as well —and I had the staff cut the overhead lights and key the music.

Cody, it was AWESOME! I WAS AWESOME!!

To the orchestrated song, "The Flight of the Bumblebee," (that chaotic and rapidly changing music that simulates the flying pattern of a bumblebee) in the pitch dark and with TWO of my LED yoyos going at once and glowing in the dark like shooting stars across a black sky, I did my best moves in time to the fast music.

I did the Gravity Pull, the Sleeper, a Forward Pass, and Breakaway. I did Rock the Baby and Pinwheel — my yoyo moving faster and faster and never messing up once. I amazed the crowd with the Lindy Loop, Time Warp, and Brain Twister. And just when I thought I was going to have a full-blown hand spasm in my right hand, I wowed the crowd with my finale — a two-handed, reverse Around the World, using alternating hands.

The crowd went NUTS!!! Absolutely nuts. Clapping and yelling and stamping their feet when I'd finished. (But I can't take ALL the credit for their excitement. That song is super overstimulating, and by then, everyone was pretty much jacked up on Mountain Dew and s'mores.)

Guess what? I won Second Place! I even received a plastic trophy and a red ribbon to pin on my shirt. First Place went to the Pixie Hollow girls and their Cirque du Soleil act. (Things that make you go hmmm.... Those outfits were a tad skimpy if you ask me, and the boy judges outnumbered the girls 2 to 1.)

Cody, this is the last letter that you'll receive from me. I don't know if I'm happy or sad about that. I'm happy that I'll get to see you in person when we meet up at the beach this summer, but I'm sad that I'll no longer get to hang out in my cabin with my newfound friends and write to you while below me they laugh and sing and play games — sometimes with me joining along.

We have this big poster on the back wall of our cabin. It's a quote by Misty Copeland (She's the first African-American female principal dancer with the American Ballet Theater.), and now that I've had these weeks at camp, I believe it to be true:

> "Anything is possible when you
>
> have the right people there
>
> to support you."
>
> ~Misty Copeland

See you soon.

XOXOX,

Willa

CAMP NEWS

August 21, 9:40 P.M.

Dear Marley,

I'M COMING HOME!

I have so MUCH to tell you, Mar, like how I realized that I'm not a hopeless loser and how I now know that I have talent AND coordination... in SOME areas. (I still tripped over my shoelaces twice today.) I also found out that once kids got to know me, they didn't seem to mind that I'm an OCD nerdy girl who recites useless trivia and remembers her daily life beginning a million years ago. (That would be in mosquito time. In human time, it's 12 years, 5 months, 1 week, 4 days, and 7 hours ago.)

I'm going to miss camp. I can't believe how right you were when you said that once I got over my fears of the "unknown," I'd learn to love it. As always, you were spot on!

Thanks for your encouragement of my relationship with Luna. There's not many BFFs who are generous enough to allow room for a new person to "stand in her stead," as you put it. And thank you again for sending me your mom to be my weekend mom for Parents' Weekend. For that, and so much more than words can say, I'll be forever grateful.

With much love,

Willa

August 21, 9:45 P.M.

Dear Dad,

This will be my last letter to you from camp, and it will probably come in the mail AFTER I get home so don't tell me when you get it, OK? (Because that will be really embarrassing if you're reading it when I'm around.)

You asked me in your letter what I learned from my first — and hopefully NOT last — camp experience. Well, here goes.

I learned that staying in one's comfort zone can stunt our emotional AND our physical growth.

I learned that it's OK to fail, but that it's important to try. I also learned that everyone is good at something even if they don't know it yet.

I learned that "dirt don't hurt" and that mud

can help relieve the pain from mosquito bites.

I learned that, yes, bears do poop in the woods (because I stepped in some more than once) and no, a one-legged duck does not swim in circles.

I learned that Dorothy was right when she said, "There's no place like home," but that camp can bring wonderful new experiences and create lasting friendships.

But maybe what I learned most of all — as a FORMERLY shy girl who was afraid of making new friends — is that sometimes saying goodbye is even harder than saying hello.

See you soon.

Love,

Willa

More Nerdy Girl Books by Linda Rey

TOP SECRET:
Diary #1 (Confessions of a Nerdy Girl)

UNLUCKY THIRTEEN:
Diary #2 (Confessions of a Nerdy Girl)

NERDY EVER AFTER:
A Nerdy Novel, Book 1 (Confessions of a Nerdy Girl)

NERDY GIRLS DON'T:
A Nerdy Novel, Book 2 (Confessions of a Nerdy Girl)

To see all of Linda's titles for younger readers visit her website at www.LindaReyBooks.com and www.NerdyGirlBooks.com

SAMPLE CHAPTER

Confessions of a Nerdy Girl:

TOP SECRET, Diary #1

March 1, 7:09 P.M.

~~Dear Diary,~~

Ugh! That looks even dumber on paper than it sounds out loud.

~~Dear Journal,~~

Nope.

~~Dear Ledger,~~ Definitely not. Too CPA-ish.

Notebook? Chronicle? Log? (Log? That's ripe. What is this—Star Trek?)

Who would ever think it's this hard to begin a diary? The chances of this thing working out are pretty slim if I can't get past the first two words. And even if I figure out what to name you — you are a "you" right? Isn't that why I'm supposed to start off with a greeting ... Dear so and so, because you're like some imaginary or invisible friend? Then what? I pour out all the details of my crappy life so I can get even more depressed when I see it all in black and white? As if living through it in real time isn't bad enough?

Maybe I'm looking at this the wrong way. Maybe having a diary is supposed to be more like I'm talking to myself, a way for my conscious to communicate with my subconscious or something. If that's the case, then I guess I should start off with the words, "Dear Me."

Oh my GOSH! I am sooo overthinking this! But then I'm clinically OCD, so I overthink everything. Who CARES what I start with? It's a diary for Pete's sake, not a Master's thesis.

This book even has a corny pastel cover that says WARNING! DO NOT READ! PRIVATE PROPERTY! (which of course just begs it be read by any Tom, Dick or Harry, or in my case, my sister Olivia.) It even comes with the prerequisite lock and key, which is a total joke because it's so flimsy any five-year-old with a paperclip could pick it.

My dad (he's actually my adoptive dad, but he's real to me) gave me this diary because he says he's noticed a change in me, and not for the better I'm guessing, and he thought that if I got my feelings out on paper maybe I'd get a better sense of "perspective." See things in a "different light."

He's right about the change. There'd be a change in you too if your dad came home one day and told you to start packing your stuff because the family was moving to Huntington Beach, California, in two months.

Now, I know what you're thinking: California!

The beach! Whoo hoo! Sunshine. Surfing. Bikinis. Tanned legs and blond highlights in your hair. Cute boys on skateboards, or surfboards, or boogie boards. But as they say at the Italian restaurant around the corner of my house when you ask for cheddar cheese to put on your spaghetti— fuggedaboutit.

First off, I hate the sun and it's fair to say the feeling is mutual. Ten minutes in the sun and my paper-white skin gets lobster red, until eventually it peels off in gross tissue-sized layers leaving behind, wanna guess? More white skin.

Second, I have astigmatism, so I wear thick glasses and can't see worth a darn without them, and I know for a fact the Pacific Ocean has sharks. I also know it has dolphins, but without my glasses (and maybe even with them) I'd be hard-pressed to tell the difference. A fin is a fin is a fin, especially when the saltwater is burning the crapola out of your half-blind retinas.

Third, I try NOT to go around half-naked in public because of all the hair on my arms and legs. It's black and long, and against my white skin ... Well, I'm sure you get the unattractive picture. Diane—my adoptive mom (who will never be real to me) won't let me shave my legs until next year.

She says she didn't let Olivia, her gorgeous but insanely evil daughter, shave until she was in middle school, so I can't either. I argued that in Olivia's case it didn't matter because Olivia has blond hair on her head and no visible hair anywhere on her body. Unlike me, who has to wear jeans and long sleeved shirts even during the hot humid summers in Chicago to cover up my gorilla limbs.

My argument got me nowhere if you don't count the trip to my room for an "attitude adjustment,"

(the seventh-grade version of time-out.) 😔

Fourth, ...

Forget fourth. Three's enough. Honestly, I could come up with about a hundred reasons why I don't want to move, but I'm running out of room on the page, plus I really have to pee.

Until next time,

Willa

P.S. Don't expect XOXO or hearts. I'm not that kind of person.

155

ABOUT THE AUTHOR

Linda Rey

Linda Rey was born with the voice of an angel and a brain so amazing she'll probably donate it to science. When she's not busy *fa la la-ing* from the hilltops or doing fantastical brain stuff in laboratories, Linda can be found at her computer channeling her inner tween.

To see all of Linda's titles for younger readers visit her website at www.LindaReyBooks.com and www.NerdyGirlBooks.com, or you can email her at linda@lindareybooks.com (And yes, that's her real email. Unless you don't have something nice to say, then no, it's not.)

Made in the USA
Las Vegas, NV
12 November 2023

80724316R00094